# A Bag for Life

My friend Penny is funny. She's really funny. In fact, I'd go so far to say she's one of the funniest people I've ever met. She's got a good job, nice flat, loads of friends. She's got everything a girl needs to be happy in this life one might think. The two things that would make Penny's life complete are a steady boyfriend and some steady weight-loss. She, like most of us in this country nowadays is on the heavy side of her ideal weight. She also does love a drink and is extremely partial to a cake as well so...Well let's just say she's not entirely happy with her figure but not enough to give that much of a shit that she'd do anything about it!

"Big bird, then is she?" I'm having a pint with Dougie two tums an old single friend of mine. "Charming! How do you know she's *a big bird* as you so eloquently put it?" I'm having a slight go at playing Cupid tonight. I'm trying to set Penny up with my mate Doug, who's single, funny and loves his food and drink. Consequently, Doug is also on the heavier side of the scale. He has however professed the need to;

"Meet a soulmate to love, laugh and eat with obviously"

"Well? Well? How big is she? Why won't you tell me, you know I'm a fan of the larger lady. Bigger the cushion the better the..."

"Please! Please. Do not finish that revolting sentence. It makes you sound like more of a dick than you actually are, if that were possible. What is it with you? Why would you think Penny is a fat bird and more's to the point why would you care?"

"Well my friend. I guess it's because you describe her as *"one of the funniest people I know"*

Now, you and I both know the old adage about people, *only being funny if they're fat"*

There's absolutely no way I can admit to that, despite me perhaps, previously agreeing in part and also whilst drunk mind, with that as a broad rule of comedy.

"I never fucking said that ever you knob!" I lie, easily.

"Ergo if she's really funny..."

"Oh fuck off! Ergo? Ergo my nut sack and ergos me as well"

I'm happy with this lame pun as a parting shot and take my leave of the cretin pausing only to spill his last dribble of beer in his lap and give him a dead arm so he doesn't miss me too much until we meet again.


Penny has had a mixed bag of dates in recent times. It's not that she's short of male attention rather than she'd like to meet someone who...

"Liked me for myself and wasn't either some weird feeder type or a chubby chasing sex maniac"

There must be masses of willing candidates? Not so according to our Penny who to her credit is regaling us in sordid detail of the latest failed meeting.

"It was all going so well, he seemed to be keen and I liked him enough to go back to his flat anyway so…One thing led to another and we were getting a bit saucy on his sofa. We were going to definitely be making the beast with two backs in a matter of minutes. So, I went to the bathroom to freshen up leaving Del to;

"Get ready for you in the bedroom Princess"

"Princess!" I guffaw my delight at this. None of the present company are what could be described as romantic or prone to much in the way of mushy pillow talk but Penny takes an exceedingly dim view of that sort of nonsense.

"Stick your Mills and Boon bollocks where the sun don't shine" she's often been heard to utter when confronted with any hearts and flower type shenanigans.

"Anyway there I am having a tinkle, giggling a bit 'cos I've had a sherry and also, *Princess!* I don't get called that very often I can tell you. I finish off and head for the bedroom to enter the fray. Words can't really do justice to the scene I found before me people. Bear with though and I'll try. Del...I presume it's Del as his face is covered. Del is lying face down; he's handcuffed to the bedposts"

The room dissolves into raucous laughter but is quietened at once by Penny's raised hands and stern expression.

"Hush now folks. That was in no way the most disturbing part of the technicolour picture painted entirely in blue before my poor eyes..." We gasp in mock anticipation, I'm nearly wetting myself, she does tell a good tale does Penny.

"Laid out next to him on the bed is a fairy princess outfit, a large one obviously before you say anything, and out of his bottom is sticking one half of the biggest dildo I've ever set eyes on!"

That's too much for me. I can hardly breathe I'm laughing so hard. I fear I've bust a rib and I'm begging Penny to stop, no chance.

"This fucker's a yard long I swear! And, blue! The fucking sick bastard!"

"Well what did you do?" the wife chimes

"Well I did what any self-respecting princess would do..."

"So what, you popped the costume on and took a seat on the blue avenger then?" I politely suggest

"Did I heck as like! I got my shit together pronto and high tailed it out of there. I did give the old blue double ender a good kick on my way out for good measure mind, he fair squealed like a little piggy. Oooh it was horrible"

Penny regales the gathered friends with another tale before declaring;

"Right I'm off, I've booked an hour in the gym tonight I've got a hot date tomorrow and I wanna look my best!

"Shall we get another drink somewhere else Penny?" Clint asks hopefully, he really likes this girl.

"That'd be great!" Penny, trying not to sound too keen, failing and not caring. He's adorable and she's got a warm fuzzy feeling inside and just for once it's not down to Southern Comfort and Baileys.

"I said shall we go then? You were off in a bit of a day dream then" Clint smiles, oh God what a smile! Calm down Pen, Jesus, get a grip girl.

Clint is holding her coat for her to put on. Like a proper gentleman would! He's almost too good to be true.

They make their slightly tipsy way up the corridor to Clint's plush docklands apartment. Penny cannot believe her luck here. He's handsome, charming and rich apparently!

"Mother *would* be pleased...as long as I play it coooool...Sorry what was that?"

Penny snaps back into the present.

"You said something about your mother"

Clint smiling again eyebrows raised quizzically.

"Oh God I'm sorry Clint I was just thinking how much my mum would like this place. She loves a bit of glass modernist does mother."

Clint chuckles and pops the cork from a bottle of Cristal! Fucking Cristal! He must be minted. What's wrong with this bloke?

Penny's waiting for Jeremy Beadle to jump out to end the prank, or for the spell to be broken somehow and for this picture-perfect evening to go the way of so many others and end ignominiously and in tears...

"Wow…."

"Oh. My. God!"

Penny and Clint lay drenched in their own sweat after an intense, extended bout of steamy lovemaking. Neither of them can quite believe what's just occurred. For Penny, this has been the greatest night of her adult life and as she stares into Clint's deep blue eyes she thinks, she hopes, perhaps she sees the same thoughts reflected.

Clint stares back. This girl! This great sexy funny girl! What can she see in little old Clint? What a night! Maybe this could be the start of something. Just take it nice and easy boy, no pressure. Play it cool.

Penny opens her eyes and for a second or two is unsure of her surroundings. She's brought back to the here and now as the door opens and in bowls Clint dressed in a killer suit complete with breakfast tray.

Is she still asleep? Is she dreaming all this?

"Hey beautiful, I hope you like your bacon well done, well a bit burnt if I'm honest?"

Maybe not to everyone, but to Penny those words were the most fantastic she'd ever heard. This Adonis, who made such sweet, slow and amazingly tender love to her until the early hours. Until she literally cried in ecstasy. This, this...Clint! He only likes his bacon crispy as well.

"Look, I know this may seem a bit forward but I really like you Penny. I mean I really like you and, well, I've gotta run now but can I see you again, maybe go for dinner tonight

Calm down dear, don't blow it now play it cool Penny dear.

"I'd bloody love it Clint, yes please, absolutely!" Shit, could have been cooler perhaps.

Clint beams.

"Really? Great, oh that's great! Then, like I say I must dash, got an early deadline to sort but take your time, leave the washing up I'll do it when I get back in at lunchtime and I'll bell you later ok?" He bends to give her a sweet kiss on the forehead and leaves.

He leaves her in a state of utter bliss.

Penny finishes her breakfast and gets dressed. She gets the detritus of the evening together and piles it on the dining room table ready to wash up. It's the very least she can do after being so totally spoilt. Oooh hang on a mo. Penny is taken aback by a bit of a dizzy spell. She's a little hungover maybe but really the feeling is one she's not experienced before. Her heart's beating a little fast and she's got what feels like swallows flying around in her tummy. She thinks of Clint and the night's events and her heart speeds still more. What is this...?

"I don't half need a poo!"

She did as well and disaster has struck. Penny has laid a cable too big to be flushed. On looking down and seeing this russet behemoth she at first starts to chuckle. The chuckle turns into a full-blown cackle as she marvels at the sheer size of the thing. She presses the button to flush her leavings goodbye and ceases to laugh. It will not go down. It refuses to leave. That's ok, Penny is a woman of the world and not to be defeated she searches for a toilet brush with which to encourage the errant shit on its journey to the coast.

"Bugger! No loo brush. He's not perfect after all!" Penny smirks to herself thinking if that really is Clint's only fault then as far as she's concerned its game on for the Penny and Clint show.

Penny heads back into the dining room and moves the rubbish to the kitchen keeping an eye out for some kind of implement to break up the unwanted guest in the bathroom. She washes the dishes, wipes down the surfaces and gets the flat looking spotless apart from the elephant in the room (huge turd in the bog). The flat is beginning to stink a bit now and Penny is panicking slightly.

Understandably mind, she has just disgraced herself rather by depositing two foot of fetid sausage as thick as an otter halfway down her new beau's U-bend.

There's nothing else for it. She must seize the bull by the horns as it were. She's found a Waitrose bag for life under the kitchen sink and this will enable her to grasp her turd safely and take it with her to dispose of (admittedly not completely satisfactorily) in the apartments communal bins outside. Satisfied it's a workable plan Penny collects her belongings and heads off retching slightly into the bathroom.

"Oh God...Blurch...Hwep...Ooof ohmygod Aaaaaaaaah!" it's easily the worst thing Penny has ever had to do but with no other option available she carries out the task, literally, in hand.

Penny places the bag with its horrific contents momentarily on the dining room table as, still retching she heads off back into the bathroom to scrub her hands clean. She takes a notepad from her handbag and writes;

"Until tonight darling, can't wait to see you again, X X X P"

Note left, flat tidied, washing up done, check. Penny shuts the door noting the sound, a reassuringly expensive and secure sounding thud.

Inside the flat a Waitrose bag for life sits on the dining room table.

Penny is still hoping to hear from Clint

# Miss Planet

Dai Evans, floor manager, 58 years old, likes a laugh, loves a drink.

He's a lovely guy and very funny. He's worked for the Miss Planet organisation for fifteen years and has had to put up with all the foibles of the cretinous Worley family. These range from the sexual predation of Ernest until his timely (and most who knew him would say his welcome) death. Through to the sweaty lipped, bumbling ineptitude of his odious progeny Martin. They also come via the outright bitchiness of Cruella de Ville as she known by the crew or Julie as her mother named her.

For suffering these fools for so long Dai Evans deserves a medal at least.

It may sound like a dream job to the uninitiated but herding 130 beautiful, pampered young ladies around the world has its own, unique set of challenges.

One can only guess at the full desperate list of demands laid at the feet of the unfortunate Welshman.

Like I say Dai really is a lovely guy with a ready wit and charm to spare. He would need all this on the last occasion I saw him whilst filming Miss Planet in London's Excel centre. The catering arrangements at the Excel can be most politely described as poor. In this scenario I prefer to cut out the middle man, throw my free food from house caterers straight into the bin, then walk the mile to the nearest pub.

It's as a result of this I find myself with Dai, Stu, John and a couple of others in the Intrepid Fox. We've all got a pint and if not cordon bleu, then at least an edible meal in front of us and Stu is egging on Dai to tell us one of his many tales of woe relating to his globetrotting job.

Dai doesn't need much persuading to be honest and he's particularly keen to tell us of his recent visit to Mongolia where,

"I'd obviously tried some of the local delicacy, well you have to don't you?"

"I bloody didn't" chimes in Stu the lighting director who travels with Dai to all these events.

"Fermented goat's milk, I ask you? What kind of idiot falls for that?" Stuart adds

Yep, Dai

"I didn't fall for anything you bugger. The only thing that did fall, rather unfortunately was my arse out of my trousers!" He guffaws loudly at this and Stu goes slightly green in the gills at the memory of Dai farting badly in the holding area backstage at the show. In fact, the resulting stench was so bad the hall manager was summoned and a team of workers despatched to check the state of the sewers servicing the hall.

"Miss Guam was actually sick!" Dai laughs wheezily and is struggling to get his breath so hard that Stuart finishes the tale with a blunt "And then he shat himself!"

That stops Dai laughing.

Dai stands up slowly from the table folds his napkin and exclaims

"I don't think I've ever been so embarrassed or betrayed in my entire life Stuart"

This is awkward. We all stare at our phones and avoid making eye contact with the antagonists. Stu's mouth is opening and closing slowly in unison with the sad, shocked, shake of Dai's grizzled head.

"HA! Hahahahahahahahaha" Dai and Stu dissolve into what can best be described as a fit of schoolboy giggles.

"Ooooh your face Crockers, bless you. As if me and him would fall out because of a little thing like that." Scratching his arse in homage to this shameful memory Dai shuffles off to the bar and orders another

"Brace of ales!"

Pair of twats they are, fair play though they had us all going there. I give Stu and Dai the finger on the way out the door and take the boys back to work. We leave them to revel in the warm glow of the tiny gag they just pulled.

Stu and Dai don't re-appear for another couple of hours and are trying and failing to keep a low profile. Giggling like a pair of errant teenage girls they sit out at the front of house position bathed in the warm fug of a five-pint lunch and the decidedly less pleasant fug of Dai's arse gas.

We finish our work for the day and arrange to meet Stu back in the hall at 8 am the next day.

As arranged the lighting crew are in at 8am and ready to work.

9am...ready to work, no sign of Stuart.

9:30.

"Morning chaps, sorry about the slightly late appearance. Me and Dai had a sherry or two in the bar last night. Where is the old sod anyway? Anyone seen him?"

We shake our collective head

"Not seen him yet Stu, no" I confirm.

Just then we're greeted by the sight of a puffing Dai Evans striding purposefully towards us at the control position.

"Morning Dai!" I shout hoping to stir his fuzzy head up a touch "All good in the hood?"

"Never mind that" He's shaking his hands, fingers pointing to the sky in a state of high excitement.

"You will never believe what's just happened to me fellas!"

...Well I might hazard a guess but the man is clearly busting to tell us and who am I to deny him?

"Stu and I had about ten pints in the bar last night and, well, to put not too fine a point on it I was fucking shitfaced! Blimey I didn't know which end was up so to speak, so I was relieved to find myself back in my room safe and warm when I woke up this morning. Bit late down for breakfast but no harm done. So anyway, there I am full of sausage, eggs, bacon, the full monty as it were, bloody marvellous it was as well. However just as I'm finishing off I feel a familiar bubbling from the basement area and well, bearing in mind my record in the trouser department, think it wise if I remove myself from the eating arena and back upstairs for a turn out pronto!"

Again, our collective head starts to shake as this sadly predictable tale unfolds before our ears.

"Well, all was great until bloody Miss France asked me for a hand with her suitcases. Fuck knows what she keeps in there but I'll not be lifting them again I can tell you. I get in the lift with her and a few of the other girls and Chris the sound man and press 7 for my floor. Miss France is only going up to the mezzanine floor and asks if I can;

"Elp me wiz ze case to ze room Cherie?"

"I know I said I wouldn't lift it again but she asked so sweetly and I am a gentleman so obviously, I agreed. Unfortunately, when I bent down to pick it up, well, to be brutally honest, I let myself down again! That caused a bit of chaos in the lift I can tell you. I was nearly killed by the stampede. Some of the language as well, shameful! They were quite upset I can tell you, Miss France is insisting I pay for new luggage and the dry cleaning of her slippers, I ask you?  What about me? It took me an hour to clean that lift up and worse still I had to throw those shorts straight in the bin, thirty quid they were, they were only a month old"

Dai Evans is still employed by the Miss Planet organisation and no contestants were hurt in the telling of this tale.

# Jasper, Slurried

Brian is on his eighth pint of Guinness, its half
past nine. He's been in the pub since five o
clock. He'll be going for a curry with the boys
later so he'd better leave some room for that
cos you have to have a couple of scoops with
a ruby, don't you?

Brian is five foot two in his socks and if one
were to be able to measure him around the
waist I'd not be surprised to discover he's as
broad as he is long.

He's a builder, a fine one at that and he lives
in his self-built ranch style house
'Caso Meo' proclaims the sign above the
door.

"It means my house in Spanish" well nearly
anyway.

This lays off the main road in the well to do commuter belt town of Kings Langley. I know Pincher through his son Fitz, (we'll meet him again later) and he's quite a character its true to say. I say the house lays off the main road but you wouldn't know it was there had you not been shown it. This is because, according to Fitz, Brian built it without planning permission and if it manages to go undiscovered by the council for another year it can stay up and they can

"Go fuck 'emselves the feckin shysters!"

The subject came up one drunken evening when whilst stood in his kitchen I realised I could easily place my palm on the ceiling. I say, it was built that way because it was as high as they could reach without hiring scaffolding but apparently, it was for the reason stated above. Fitz claimed never to have noticed the low ceilings before...he ain't the tallest either to be fair.

"Another one Brian?"

The barman is already pouring Brian's ninth pint. There's no reason to believe he'll not be having his usual ten or eleven.

"Better give him a large Jimmy in there as well" Patrick chimes in

"He's drinking like a bit of a girl today sure enough" Paddy agrees

"Even if I was a girl I'd still be able to drink you two pricks under the table and I'd still have a bigger langer an all!" Brian dissolves into a wheezing bout of hilarity at his own joke getting increasingly louder and coughing more, until ending abruptly by farting and exclaiming,

"Ooof fuck me I think I'm touching cloth here" and making haste to the bathroom. "That'll itch when it dries out I reckon" Says Patrick sagely.

"Alright Mahat?! Three Cobras, ten mixed poppadum's one lamb tikka, onion bajis, chicken jalfrezi, garlic naan special fried rice sag aloo chana chat and whatever the other twats are having. Hahahahaha"
"Certainly Mr Brian, same as usual, so nice to see you again (you fat bastard)
Islam Mirza has run the local Indian restaurant for ages and is used to the casual racism employed by his customers as a rule but after serving Brian every other night for seven years, him calling him Mahat Macoat is wearing thinner by the minute. Tonight, I

think Mr Brian I may grind up some of my finest Naga chillies and give you something to truly remember me by. Islam is finally off at the end of the month. He's going to take his savings and finally and go home to live life in peace in his beloved Punjab surrounded by his family and friends and not by fat fucking racist peasants.

Fast forward 2 hours.

Whump! Brian's van rams into the concrete post by the front door. It's almost as if he made this feature especially sturdy for exactly this sort of occasion. He probably runs into it twice a week so perhaps it's just as well it was built to last.

The alarm is trying its best but in reality, has little chance of waking Brian.

Fifteen pints and £50 worth of curry makes for a heavy sleep and no mistake.

It's only the fact that Fitz is leaving for work at Seven and has to move Brian's Van out of the front garden that alerts him to his dad's lie in.

"Come on fatty get out your pit and get your fat arse to work!"

Fitz know this is unlikely to rouse his beloved father from his slumber.

He also knows that the pint of cold water he then throws at him undoubtedly will. He's out the door and in his own van with the engine running as Brian appears naked at the front door with a promise to

"Tear you a new arsehole when I get my hands on you!"

Fitz gives his dad the middle finger and with a well-worn cry of

"Unlucky loser!" disappears off up the main road.

Brian's in a rush now. He's well late and he had to be at Holland Park at the Glendenning extension job an hour ago. No time for a shit shave or shower today, he'll just have to suck it up and power through the day ahead. With any luck those other fuck tards will be on time and able to cover for him. He is the boss after all and is owed a certain level of respect surely? He doesn't get much at home that's for fucking sure.

Brian manages to find his van in the garage eventually, fuck knows how it got there he thought he'd parked it in the drive? He sets off on his merry way and is only twenty minutes in to the journey when the first deep rumble raises a chuckle.

"Pwoar I reckon that old portaloo is in for a bit of a bashing later" He laughs to himself. Brian is, like most men, still anally fixated or to put it in simpler turns in love with the fart gag and all things shit related. That was just one of a long list of things that Jenny his ex could not put up with.

"Miserable cow" he mutters in memory. Another low growl from the bowel brings a smile but this time there's just a slight hint of worry as his already ample tummy seems slightly larger than usual this morning. Squeeeeeeeak!

"What the fuck?" Brian exclaims as another bizarre noise issues forth from the depths of his digestive tract.

He's just passed the last services on the way in so he'll have to wait until he gets into town now. At least the traffic will have died down a bit as he's so late.

Thank God for small mercies he thinks. With a bit of luck, he'll be there within the hour and relief will be swift and welcome.

He manages to get to Holland Park in an hour so is just the two hours late today something Lady Glendenning has had to become used to. He parks over the road next to the park entrance and hobbling now due to the distended state of his gut and the massive faecal package bearing down on his ring piece makes his way to the portaloo. Where's the portaloo gone?

"Paddy! Paddy! Where's the shit house to?" He shouts urgently.

"Cracked it with the forklift yesterday Brian remember? It's been picked up and there'll be another here in an hour supposedly" Paddy tries not to laugh at the shuffling Brian. He's clearly in some discomfort, holding his gut with one hand and his arse with the other

"An hour! I haven't got a minute let alone an hour you fucking bollocks"

"You'll have to go in the house Bri" Chirps Patrick before adding through clenched teeth and splitting sides "Oh fuck no you can't can you? Coz Mrs G has taken Jasper out for his morning doings"

"You'll have to use the one in the park then"
says Paddy "I'd get a wriggle on though boss,
that looks serious!"

Brian is in agony now which makes it all the
more amusing for the on looking duo. He's
affecting the waddling, stumbling gait of the
man in imminent danger of shitting his pants
and makes his way sweatily and swearing
heavily into the park.

"Ooof, oooh fuck me. Jaysis...c'mon now
Brian you can make it. C'mon Brian another
minute and all will be well c'mon now boy
concentrate"

It's going to happen, all will be well. Brian is a
matter of seconds and yards away from the
public convenience situated just inside
Holland Park.

Hold up though, what does that say? No, it can't be. Brian can hardly read the words on the notice pinned to the door so hard is he concentrating on keeping his anal sphincter clamped firmly shut. Read though he does and understand he must, the most chilling of phrases;

## Closed for re-furbishment

That's torn it.

Brian is mere moments away from a cataclysmic event the like of which is likely to rent his bum asunder.

The bushes, the bushes, the bushes are his only option. Barely able to move now he forces his legs, one step...two step..." Oh God oh God, Oh sweet Jesus.

Brian starts to unbuckle his belt as he makes his way inexorably but painfully slowly into the undergrowth.

"Jasper!

Jaaaaaasssssspaaaah!

Mrs Glendenning is, as we know, taking her beloved Springer spaniel for their morning walk to enable him to do him business and to get some badly needed exercise. He's a lovely dog no doubt, all be it a bit on the tubby side from tit bits and not enough walkies. Brian loves him as well and he knows when he sees him he's in line for a treat of some sort or another.

Jasper circles excitedly around Brian's feet awaiting his treat

Brian hovers above his...

"Fuck off Jasper for Christs' sake he utters with his last ounce of energy before...

Woosh Jasper rushes back towards his owner between Brian's legs

QUAAAAAACKSHHHHHPLAT

Brian voids himself. The relief is immense, orgasmic almost. Brian looks down.

Oh good God

"Jasper! Here pretty pretty"

Jasper is on the floor. Jasper has been dropped there by the high-powered shit spray visited on him from above. In short he's been slurried. Rotting faecal matter drips from every hair as he makes his reeking vomiting way from the undergrowth.

"Jasper? Jasper! Oh, Jasper, what have you rolled in?" Says Mrs G before throwing up all over her Guccis.

Paddy and Patrick managed to finish the job on their own eventually.

Brian was not welcome back apparently.

# Mr Mead is on the Dancefloor

We de-camp from the Metropolis to the wild
of the Somerset levels.

We have been engaged to light and dress and
therefore enhance immeasurably, the 60th
birthday of a Mr Mead.

Its 1994 and the second summer of love is
but a distant memory.

Bold new labour has been shown to be staid
old Tories and the world is creaking along
with itself. Eastern Europe coming apart and
together at once, whilst the USA and Russia

look on greedily awaiting the next chance to meddle.

I've been side tracked here, my apologies. Mr Mead. It transpires that our client for the next 3 days was one time affianced to 4$^{th}$ in line horse faced royal Princess Anne. She of the famously buck toothed ability to eat an apple through a tennis racquet.

We drive for hours and eventually what seems like miles up a winding drive in our trusty wobble wagons to be halted in view of an impressive looking mansion by a frantically waving green wellied lady.

"No no no. Stop stop stop. What an earth are you doing?" She cries desperately.

I'm driving and as I'm in her direct line of fire I take it upon myself to get involved before our glorious leader Laz in the following van.

"Running you over nearly luv" I say in what I imagine is my best cheeky/charming cockney tone.

"Round the back! Round the back with you! Heavens above Sir will not be happy if you churn up the front with your dirty work vans"

"I'd churn up her front no worries" Chimes Pablo but she doesn't hear or either chooses not to let us know she's heard.

"Turn around immediately, go back to the gate house and turn right. Go into the village and take the first right as you leave. The tradesman's entrance is a mile down on the right. I'll join you around the back"

"I'd join her round..."

"Shut up Pablo" Jesus! Pablo is stuck firmly in Benny hill/Bernard Manning territory when it comes to women.

"At least wait until we find out who she is before you offer to

"Knock her back doors in" or "Check out her plumbing" will you please Pab?"

"Bender!" He laughs as I turn the van around, driving onto the grass in doing so and sending Wellybird into an apocalyptic shit fit in the process.

As we wheel spin back off up the drive we pebble dash the poor woman totally. Adding this to the list of apparently major transgressions already committed and we can safely say this job has not had the most auspicious of starts.

Laz flashes his lights as we reach the gate house and we get out of the vans for a team talk.

I appraise him of our brief conversation with the irate lady and he rightfully decides that he should head up the next approach to the venue. He also rightfully advises Pablo to keep on the side of shtum in order to preserve any chance we have of seeing this job through and getting paid thereafter.

On our way through the village a quaint little pub catches our collective eye and seeing as how the sun is very nearly over the yard arm the decision is made to have lunch at early doors. The pub is already quite full at midday and whilst I don't claim it fell into a "High Noon" silence as we entered, the volume certainly dropped enough to make us uncomfortable. We've walked in and out of a lot unfriendlier places than this however and unbowed the five of us bowl up to the bar.

Rick Gallop makes up another of our quintet and sporting one eyebrow, one half of a beard and the other half of a moustache breezily orders

"Five pints of wife beater my good fellow and a portion of whatever takes your fancy to boot while you're at it!"

The barman looks all bar dumbfounded by this and sensing this Rick continues.

"I know I'm a stranger to these parts my man but unless I miss my guess English would still be the mother tongue in this environ? I shall take your silence as affirmation in this instance and ask you attend my order with no further delay!"

He delivers this all with a wide grin but due to his unusual shaving preference allied to his six feet five stick insect build he can come across as slightly intimidating.

"Five Stellas mate" I interject and the barman snaps into life.

The round arrives, is duly dispatched and another ordered without incident and Laz points out that by the time we've eaten we'll be in the realms of two to three hours late. Agreeing, we decide to skip the food and just have one more Stella.

"Eating's cheating after all!" Pipes up Shag the Fifth and last of our happy band.

Shag is the only one of us who would feel remotely comfortable in the higher echelons of society. He attended a good public school and has what can be described a "cut glass accent" That said he has, like the rest of our gang a weakness for the baser side of nature and it is this upon which our firm friendship was born.

Adequately refreshed and in truth a tad tipsy (Laz was persuaded into a fourth pint) we head off back to the "big house" as the locals call it.

As previously stated we have been employed via Laz's company Eventual Lighting to provide a lighting rig to enhance the festivities of one of our landed gentry. I'm not a fan of these types to be fair and am expecting treatment akin to that of a servant for the whole time of our engagement. That notwithstanding I'm always polite and prepared to take everyone I meet at face value.

We're met after what must be a mile long drive up a largely unmade road by

"Tippi Cooke-Palmerston PA to Mr Mead and God as far as you lot are concerned for the duration of your engagement"

Hahaha...well I laughed. Not the correct response apparently from the warlike expression adopted by TCP as she became latterly and aptly known by the collective crew.

"You will never approach from the front again as per previous instruction.

You will not and I repeat NOT enter the house unless expressly invited to do so by either myself or a member of the family.

You will use ONLY the facilities provided in the gardens.

There will be food provided, eaten in the hand twice a day and you WILL use the bins to dispose of any resulting detritus.

You will dress in smart black shirt and trousers as per instructions

You will be show ready by 18-00 tomorrow evening and any problems or concerns must be addressed to myself alone in the meantime. Is that clear?

Any questions?"

"Nein meinen Ober Stuhrer Furher Alles gut Vielen Danke!" Gallop clicks his heels together, and with a Nazi salute goose steps off round to the back of the wobble wagon and starts to unload.

"I can assure you also that any more overt displays of disrespect will not be tolerated" TCP finishes with the haughtiest sniff ever performed and disappears thorough a door into the kitchen of the house.

"Christ what a bitch" Says Laz

"I still would" Says Pablo.

Our work place for the foreseeable future is a marquee in the grounds of the "big house" As a group and individually we've done thousands of events. Between us we are well used to many different environments. Indeed, without wishing to blow our collective trumpet *too* loudly, we're very fucking good at our jobs and can adapt to most situations without too much drama. I say all this by way of explanation and not in any way to excuse some of the, frankly shocking behaviour that ensued.

The lights are up, the sound is pumping and the room is full.

This is the bare minimum required in my opinion for a successful party.

Well there are caveats I suppose. Among these I reckon that the whole party not be full to the brim of chinless twats, people called Cassandra, Cubby, Peregrine or Boris. Holy hand grenades! I can honestly say I've never been in the vicinity of such a large gathering of vacuous turds in all my life. What I will say about this lot is at least they don't mind buying drugs at exorbitant prices! A little side-line we have, is punting out illicit substances at these posh events. It enables us, or me and Pablo, to be more specific, to earn reasonably well whilst working (In our collective opinion) inordinately hard.

That said, we *are* here to work and put a party on for a bloke who's paid good money for it and deserves therefore to have a good party put on. To this end, I in my wisdom have decided that at the very least, if and when our host gets

on the dancefloor we should welcome the occasion is some small way.

Hence the first time Mr Mead arrives to check to see how proceedings are going he is greeted by a half cut me in faux Caribbean styley, howling through a loud hailer;

"MEESTA MEAD AM ON DE DANCEFLOOR!" Strobes go off and disco lights flash and Mr Mead whinnies in delight at this comedic welcome.

I've had a chat with the bar staff and mentioned to them that, well, seeing as how

their chillers are in fact powered by the
generators provided by us, they should
probably/definitely out of politeness, if not
professional necessity, keep the lighting
department liberally supplied with all and
every type of alcohol available.

Our cheer is cut short by TCP bounding over
thunder faced and yelling in my face;

"How dare you take your host's name in
vain? Who are you people? In what world do
you live where you find it acceptable, let
alone de rigeur to belittle the name of Mr
Mead?"

"Calm down dear" I think, or try to think at
least. What I'm actually thinking is

Fuck off cunt, get a grip, are you serious? and
fuck off again in no particular order.

"Triffic job chaps, bally well done all round I say. Look forward to having a snifter with you all tomorrow yeah?"

Hahahahhahaha Mr Mead loves it!

Hahahahha.

TCP looks like she dropped her canapes in a puddle.

Well I can only assume TCP did think about it as she huffed off at the speed of, if not light, then something akin to it...murk maybe, I dunno.

A brief few hours later after a sweaty night spent in an uninspiring bnb we trundle into work again. This time though, via the agreed rear entrance. That said, Pablo assured us he would

"Still show that Tippi bird the joys of full frontal access"

She'd never sleep again I'm sure, had she known exactly what Pablo had in mind.

Anyway, despite a massive collective hangover we got on with the task in hand. Trusses were rigged, lights were powered, trees were lit.

All was well and the hour of the party duly arrived as did England's finest by the Rolls load. Never before or since has such a collection of prize turds gathered under one roof. The Palmer-Tomkinsons, the Legg-Bourkes, the Shand-Kydds. I doubt one could get an invite without at least a double barrel attached. Two things I do know about the upper class mind.

1) They like their drugs
2) They have no idea how much they should cost!

These two happy facts made for a very profitable night for yours truly and also for Pablo and his lucrative cocaine business. We were very popular boys it has to be said and served up all manner of pharmaceuticals to the mass of aristos. This had a couple of immediate effects. Firstly, we made an inordinate amount of cash. Secondly the toilets got very busy due to the sniffing of and then the results of Pablo's marching powder. The crew were under strict instructions as I said not to even enter the house so we were given a builder's portaloo around the back of the marquee to use. Now I'm no snob and have not the slightest problem when it comes to having a piss. Like most men I'll happily get the little fella out point him at any vertical surface and Bob's yer uncle. However, when it comes to having a poo, I draw the line at doing it in the dark within a square metre of minging plastic. The night is moving swiftly on I've had half a pill to get me in the mood to flash lights for the revelling toffs and we're having a belly laugh watching probably the worst dancing ever witnessed en masse anywhere in the civilised world. Almost in a class of his own, mind is our host. Mr Mead jerks, twists, thrusts his cumberband in all directions at once and in a time all of his own making. At every foray onto the floor he's greeted with his personal megaphone/strobe fanfare making absolutely sure none of his moves are missed by his crowd of adoring fuckwits.

I on the other hand have to miss his next sequence as the time for a poo is upon me and its upon me in no uncertain fashion. I have a quandary. Whether to obey the strict instructions of TCP, hold my nose and brave the portaloo or to say bollocks to it and have a dump in the big house.

Obviously within minutes I'm creeping around on the first floor getting ever more desperate when eventually I come across Mr Mead's personal sheisen hausen. It's bigger than my flat and decorated in that gaudy gold and flock wallpaper so beloved of the truly rich and totally tasteless.

It's no exaggeration to say I found my goal in the very nick of time.

As soon as my bum cheeks touched down on the polished oak of Mr Mead's personal throne I dropped one of the biggest logs to ever see the light of day. It fairly roared out and at such velocity that a most unwelcome splash back soaked my bunched up jeans. I clean my ring and stare wide eyed into the pan with a mixture of horror and not a little pride at what I've managed to deposit. But, oh for fucks sake my pleasure and relief at such a successful download are soon tempered as all attempts to flush the beast are met with utter failure. I'm in a spot here and need to think fast as surely my discovery in this most hallowed of water closets, will be met with severe sanction. I decide to give it one more hard flush and muster rather too much force on the lever. There is a loud twonk! And the linkage breaks inside the cistern. There's no option but to have the lid off and have a gander inside. I grab the heavy porcelain lid and lift it carefully from its position. Fuck me they built them solid in the old days. it weighs about fifty pound. I look quickly around for a sensible place to rest it but before I can put it down I drop the fucker! Di...fucking...saster. The lid drops straight into the pan and cracks a huge hole in the bowl. My Jurassic log seizes its chance of escape and slithers off along the polished tile floor towards the door like some kind of fetid sea serpent. I watch mouth agape as the terrible scene unfolds before me. Holy shitting Armageddon what the cock am I to do now? As soon as the man of the house

feels the need to nip one off I'll be

discovered. Luckily I have on my person a

Leather man multi tool. Taking care not to

step on my former lodger I edge around it to

the door and sneak a glimpse up the hall. The

coast is clear which cannot be said for the

scene I leave behind in the cistern chapel as I

lock the door from the outside with my tool.

Leaving quietly, I tiptoe my way down the

hall and am about to make good my escape

when from a door to my left I hear,

"Oooh yes that's it, give it to me you dirty

workman!"

Hahahaha that's unmistakably TCP's voice

and unless I miss my guess Pablo is making

good on his earlier wishes to "knock her back

doors" in or some other equally charming

adage. Without further ado, I make good my exit and am back in the marquee before anyone is any the wiser.

In the ensuing steward's inquiry launched by a furious Mr Mead the next morning we were able to deny any involvement in "Shit gate" and were able to provide the alibi of having been in the company of TCP for most if not the entirety of the evening.

Happy days!

# The Baked Alaskan of Muswell Hill

I've just finished a massive corporate de-rig at the Grosvenor House Ballroom in Park Lane. It was a jolly up for Cresswell Paper. It was a terrible job, long hours and hard work made bearable solely because of an inspired piece of bullshit given to the regional sales manager by yours truly in the toilets in between courses.

"Hello mate, you're on the crew, aren't you?"

I don't usually chat to strangers in toilets contrary to any rumours you might have heard but he seems friendly enough so I nod.

"Yup, for my sins"

"Who's the after-dinner entertainment? We know it's a band and the rumour is its someone big."

I finish my piss and wash my hands.

"Listen" I say beckoning him to one side as we exit the loo.

"We've been sworn to secrecy but if you get me and the boys a bottle of red I'll tell you who it is. You've got to promise not to tell anyone else though or I'll be for the high jump"

Agreement is made, a bottle of ridiculously overpriced claret is purchased, and the lie is told...

"It's Dire Straits..."

I leave him open mouthed with shock. He's clearly a big fan of the gravel voiced middle of the road nonsense trotted out by the 1980's super group.

I take the wine up to the boys and we watch as the salesman weaves his way through the crowd telling fucking every person in the room, as I fully expected him to.

There's a ripple of excitement in the room as the CEO gets up to announce the cabaret for the evening.

"We've had a great year ladies and gents we really have. Its humbling for me to head up such a dedicated, loyal sales force as your selves. Give your selves a round of applause, come on! On your feet now you deserve it COME ON!

The room rises as one. Their boss really appreciates all their hard work and no mistake. It's a magic feeling being part of this team, part of this great company.

"And as a mark of our esteem and thanks for all this year's hard work I'd like to welcome to the stage one of England's finest bands.

They're a personal favourite of mine and I know you're gonna love them too. Give them a massive Cresswell cheer. Give it up for...The Stutz Bear Catz

Woo!

There's a stunned silence, **not** the mighty Straits but the fucking who? The Stutz Bear cunting Catz?! Fuck off!

At first it's a single bread roll that bounces expertly off the head of the drummer then a plastic bottle hits the guitarist before a hail of glasses, plates and bottles forces the stunned and bleeding Catz from the stage. A mini riot ensues and the police have to be called eventually to rescue the CEO who's locked himself in the gents to protect himself from his irate drunken sales force.

I shouldn't laugh but really, Dire Straits?
Hahahaha.

Anyway, that's how come I find myself on a
134 bus at half eleven busting for a shit.

I approach Muswell Hill Broadway, I can nip
in to the O'Neils and have a dump in there,
sweet. I get off the bus and bound up the
steps to the pub.

"Sorry mate pubs closed, times been called
ten minutes ago" The bouncer puts his hand
on my chest so I'm left in no doubt as to the
message he wants to convey.

"I don't want a drink mate I just need to take
a shit! I'm dying here" I plead

"Well you'd best fuck off home and have one
then mate cos this is a pub not a public toilet.
Cheeky twat"

He gives me a bit of a shove. If I thought for one minute that I wouldn't soil myself at even a modest amount of physical activity, I'd have planted one right on his smug beak. Discretion is very much the better part of valour though in this situation and I turn to start the mile-long trek down the hill to my flat and sanctuary. I spy a light on at Shag and Pablo's flat though, relief! Oh, hurrah for me. I walk as normally as I can over the road. It's getting painful now in truth. It feels a bit like I've got a big brown tortoise in my gut and if I'm not mistaken he's starting to poke his head out my arse.

Every step is getting progressively worse but no matter cos I'm nearly there now when my phone rings. I pull It out gingerly so as not to

dislodge my bum cheek and cause an
accident. PABLO the screen reads

"Where are you? We're in the Devvy, it's all
going off in here Shag is totally pissed and
Mitch had just battered some crusty with a
bar stool"

THEY'RE NOT IN!

I'm literally six feet from their door and
nearly sob with a mixture of panic and
disappointment. I'm less than five mins away
from a very public turn out and its imperative
I find a safe haven to get rid of the weighty
mess I'm struggling to control at the very end
of my bowel. I cross back over the road and
head down the hill in the absolute certain
knowledge that I will not get home before I
shit myself. All my effort is geared towards

clenching my arse together and not letting it open even a millimetre.

I'm walking like an emperor penguin now in a tiny shuffling gait, waddling side to side and shaking my head. My eyes are streaming from the effort and I'm whimpering from the pain. Across Woodside Road I go and glance to my left.

Someone has left their garage door open! Oh, thank you Jesus! Thank you thank you thank you. I totter in please please wait and undo my belt, please please oh God Pull down my jeans and Wallop! In one foul poop I am empty! Oh, Mary Mother of God and all the little children. Sweet, sweet orgasmic relief. I begin to look around when I catch sight of my mess. Holy Moly! I have deposited what looks like an enormous baked Alaskan, bang in the middle of this poor sod's garage. My disgust at the sight is overtaken by wonder and amusement that something quite so massive could have issued forth from a single human anus. I chuckle in amazement as I wipe my arse on a greasy J cloth handily placed within arm's reach. I breathe another huge sigh of pure joy when my reverie is cut short and I'm bathed in the stark white glare of a Range Rover's headlights.

I shudder to think of what the family of four in the 4 by 4 would think of me had I stayed around to find out. I chose instead what in the circumstances was the wisest option. I wrenched my jeans up over my barely wiped arse, mounted the bonnet and Starsky and Hutched it over the roof down the back and got on my toes.

My parting shot that they should

"Treat it like a mini roundabout" Fell on deaf

ears I suspect.

# The Throne of Doom

# Chapter 1

# Druids and Tea bags

Right, have any of you heard of the
Eisteddfodd?

Yeah?

No?

Well for those of you who haven't, it's a
"world" famous poetry festival...bit of an
oxymoronic phrase there maybe though ay?

A *"World"* famous poetry festival? Is it just me who thinks that poetry hasn't really got a place in today's society? The same society that thinks it's ok to sell newspapers full of nothing but blurry shots of some celebretard's gash taken by a fat pap as they fall out of some nightclub at fuck off o'clock on a Thursday night. The same society that spends a hundred billion pounds fighting a war thousands of miles away to keep a government in power who believe in the inalienable right of men to rape their wives'?

Then again, I am just an ill educated pikey from Kent.

Yes, Kent, the Garden of England.

The Garden of England? Well that being the case I'm from the bushes at the bottom of that garden. The bushes that back onto the dog shit covered alley where the local nonce used to hide and show his cock to your sister in exchange for a Curly Wurly. You get the picture? Anyway, my point is that no one from these sorts of places gives a fuck about poetry, except maybe those who have a vested interest in its prolonged existence i.e. poets, poets' agents, the Welsh etc. The Welsh I hear you ask? I mention them of course because the Eisteddffodd, (that's the third time I've said it and the third time I imagine I've miss-spelt it as I'm writing it) is solely of interest to Welsh language speakers ergo or ergog a goch should it be? The Welsh!

I should at this point say that I have absolutely no problem with the men/women of Harlech per se. In fact, I'm married to one and I myself have Welsh blood in me. I shall now qualify that by saying that although my mother insists she is half Welsh I know for a fact that her "Welsh" father, my maternal grandfather that is, was born in Chirk, which is in England. Near Wales yes, in Wales no. I actually suspect that her real fondness for the singing thieves of Wales stems from a none too healthy liking of the taste of coal on miners' lips. She got this when she was evacuated to North Wales during World War II. I mean, you had to get by somehow did you not? Nylon stockings didn't buy themselves now did they? Let's face it, it can't have been easy being a young London girl cooped up in a house full of lusty Welsh men. Men that because of their "vital" work in digging lumps of flammable carcinogenic shit out of a hill were unable to venture to far-flung corners of the world and have their limbs flung far from them. That may all sound like I'm being a bit harsh on my mother but since I found out that apparently, I am the product of a fucked up social experiment, performed on me by her and my father over my formative years, she's only reaping what she's sown.

Actually, thinking about it further now, she was only about ten at the time war broke out, so I'm probably erring on the harsh side but if you live by the sword, pink or otherwise, then...well you know what I'm saying.

I appear to have gone off piste a bit there but it's important that you don't just think I'm a xenophobic misogynist. No, I'm so much more hateful. I struggle sometimes to think of anything I do like...dogs I suppose...beer, I like beer. Footy! Definitely football. Though I do support West Ham and they're...well...let's just say they're shit. So even my hobby, the one distraction I have that is supposed to relax me and keep my mind occupied, annoys and disappoints me. Enough of all that navel gazing nonsense anyway, back to my point.

As I said, I'm a simple lad from the wilds of Kent on the outskirts of London. I wasted the chance of a good education spending my schooldays round various other wasters' houses inhaling glue, butane or drinking, before being expelled after interfacing one of my maths teachers' faces with a dustbin lid at the age of fifteen. Luckily nepotism was alive and kicking and a friend of my brother's gave me a start at a lighting company. After a few months learning the ropes, sweeping the warehouse and clearing up the mad owner's dog's shit, I managed to land a freelance job in the stage and television lighting industry. I toured for ten years with various bands and rock groups and enjoyed it tremendously. Six months of the year would be spent on tour buses, in the roofs of theatres or concert halls. A lot of this time being spent drunk in hotels, bars and on ferries or in airport terminals. It could be glamorous at times but more usually was a mixture of hard drink and even harder work. The job in question had come up in the quiet summer period between tours and was not the sort of job I'd normally get involved in. But beggars can't be choosers so I'd gratefully accepted the chance to travel to fuck knows where? Thence to co-ordinate the installation of a lighting rig to televise fuck knows what?

The Eisteddfod. This being the fortnight long cultural festival held annually in the principality of Wales. There are a number of pre-conditions for qualifying as an entrant. Chiefly, that you must be a Welsh speaker. You might think that this would narrow the field unfeasibly but you would be ignorant in that assumption or "Ignerrrrrrant" as the main protagonist of this tale would say. Tegwyn Jones was his name and he looked for all the world like Kriss Krisstofferson after a night on the smack. He worked as a lighting director for Daffodil TV (I swear that's what they're called) and he was also a cattle farmer in the North Walian town of Bala.

Bala was famous for two things. The first being "Teggy" its mythical *part* goat, *part* dragon, *wholly* made up, lake dwelling monster. "Teggy" was even more elusive than his more famous but equally imaginary northern cousin "Nessie". Whilst craving the attention that the sighting of a legendary aquatic behemoth would bring to the area, the locals were sadly lacking in the wherewithal department. Not even one grainy photo or blurry video exists of Teggy. Come on Wales! If you are going to invent creatures to prise open the wallets of gullible foreigners, at least have the gumption to produce a modicum of evidence, no matter how ropey! This laughably poor attempt to drum up tourism was thought up as an antidote to the second thing that Bala is famous for, namely the unfriendliness of its locals.

Now where I'm from, they like nothing better than a bit of Friday night fuckery e.g. downing eight pints of lager and then stomping on the face of the nearest bloke who's not from the actual street that your pub is located in. Yes, fuck all that racism nonsense it's *so* nineties isn't it? What I'm talking about here is regionalism but taken to the 'nth degree. *Localism* - dishing out horrendous beatings to people who are not from the same postcode as you that's where it's at nowadays. I'm not sure if many of these fuck-wits would even know what a postcode was for, other than to identify the receiver of your next pint glass. The Neanderthal Bala boys were legendary in the surrounding area.

"They come out of the fuckin' 'ills walkin sideways the bastards"

That there's a direct quote from a member of the local constabulary, I shit you not.

"They come sideways into town and bite each other's fucking ears off they do...fucking rotten they are. I won't lie"

The fact that the locals spent most of their time doing hard toil on the farm or even harder toil still, down one of the few remaining mines, meant they were fit as well as mean. That, taken with a fervent dislike of the English, was, in my experience, a bad combination. That's enough of the local history for a bit, we'll have cause to re-visit it later I assure you.

The Eisteddfod then, this age-old festival of all things Welsh.

It's run by fucking Druids would you believe? Far be it for me to slag off any specific religious group. I have a hard job taking any of them seriously enough to get very excited. The Druids...what can I tell you that you don't know already? They all wear long dresses and pointy hats. They all carry long wooden sticks, 'staffs' I think they call them. They're all men and there's not one of them I saw under eighty years old. During the whole two weeks of the festival, these bizarre critters would line up at the back of the stage in all their finery and keep a very ordered and exceptionally beady eye on the proceedings. This was to make sure there was nothing untoward occurring. They were perfectly qualified for this task as it seemed to me they were the only ones with the slightest clue what the fuck was going on! Now, bearing in mind their age, the heat and the length of time-spent upright clasping large bits of wood, we opened a book on which "Pointy" would collapse next during the proceedings. Druid Bingo if you like. It was a cruel but diverting pass time. Basically, the massed ranks of Druid on the stage would be given a number by us, which corresponded to their position as they lined up on the rostrum. The back row all carried a large flagpole, which it has to be said, looked bloody heavy for the average man let alone your typical sheet-wearing octogenarian. Factor in that we were in a massive tent in the middle of one of the hottest summers for years and... Well, asking for trouble is a phrase that springs readily to mind. Let's just say the potential for comedy quickly became apparent. Armed with our Druid lottery numbers, we, the assembled Anglo invaders, would chuckle as we watched the interminable dross meted out ad nauseum in front of us throughout the day (the twelve-hour long day!). As the acts got ever stranger; Megan the granite dancing sweetheart of Gwent, the massed choirs of Maesteg etc (all singing the same song mind!), the indecipherable poets sat in the hand carved throne and rambling on gutturally (more about that shortly). Meanwhile, our dad's army of Druids grew ever wearier and started to wilt in the merciless heat.

"C3 going down!" shouts Gus, before he realises the two back rows of the audience can hear him.

"Shhhh, SSSSSSH SSSSSSSSSSHHHHHHH!"

They hiss fiercely like a nest of Welsh vipers. Apparently, you need absolute silence to appreciate the intricacies of some oddly dressed cretin hopping up and down on a round bit of highly polished rock.

"Ooh I don't know" I counter. "A12's looking rocky, in fact...Yes! Thar she blows!"

With that and the faintest whiffle of Egyptian cotton (they're not made of hemp those dresses, too itchy by far!) the former occupier of A12 performed the Druid equivalent of a backward somersault from his lofty perch. Not only that but he took his neighbour with him in a kind of Pagan half nelson.

"The pair of 'em!" A win double for yours truly and the first of hopefully many fivers in the old sky rocket

Gawd bless the Druids! Can you say that? Would the almighty Christian God ever deign to bless a Pagan non- believer? Like I said, I'm no religious expert but I doubt it somehow. Whatever.

I am however, getting ahead of myself. I should tell you about a little incident involving Tegwyn and myself first.

## Chapter 2

### Amoebic warriors

It was hot, un-feasibly hot. Like ninety degrees for Christ sake. Me and the boys had unloaded the trucks and had worked up a fair old sweat. Four articulated lorries full of lights, cables and the aluminium truss work to hang it on. A fuck load of kit for a poetry show I can tell you. Due to some unseasonably warm weather, the inside of the tent was roasting and after a couple of hours in the sweltering atmosphere, we needed a break. We were just on the way out to the pub when Tegwyn Jones arrived and put a spanner in the works.

"No no no no no no. This won't do at all. No no no no. Where on God's green earth do you think you're all going?"

I finished counting how many "no's" that was and then appealed to the man's good nature.

"The boys are all a bit hot and bothered Tegwyn. I was just going to take them to get some water."

Well folks, as it transpired Tegwyn was a man with a very good nature but only apparently as far as his fellow countrymen were concerned. We, being English and therefore the enemy, were to be treated with barely disguised contempt.

"Don't lie to me Crockers boy!" He roared, "You're a liar! You're a *liar* from a *nation* of liars!"

Well I never! Even this most heinous of insults was rendered amusing by his outrageous pronunciation and delivery. So, trying hard not to laugh in his face, begrudgingly and much to the boy's disgust, I agreed that yes, maybe it was too soon to be having a break. Bless their little hearts! Back into the sweltering tent the boys went, pausing only briefly to register their collective displeasure with a whispered but predictable chorus of....

"Welsh prick"

"Taffy cunt"

"Fucking farmer!"

On we worked for another three baking hours and the boys were sweating and grumbling fit to burst, so I suggested to Tegwyn that maybe *now* might be an agreeable time to go for refreshments.

"Oh Diddums! Are the mighty English workers finding the going all a bit tough for them? Maybe they'd like me to fan their fevered brows with some ten pound notes to keep them cool now is it?"

I take exception to this mocking tone once again and am about to gift Tegwyn with some knowledge when I have an altogether better idea.

"How's about I make us a nice cup of tea Tegwyn ay? How'd that be? The boys can get some water down their necks and we can all take five minutes to cool down a bit"

"Oooooogggh. Tea. Now that's the first bit of sense you've made today is that boyo"

I'd make him a nice cuppa. I'd make him a cup of tea he'd never fucking forget.

I went off to make the tea and the boys all took the weight off, had some water and calmed down a bit. I gave Tegwyn his tea and watching him closely, drank my own.

"Lovely...Oooogh. That hits the spot that does. I won't lie, that's a fine brew you've made there boyo so you are good for *some*thing at least "

"Made with my heart and soul that was Tegwyn," I say, stifling a grin.

Brewster and Gus and the rest of the boys have clocked my expression and know something is going on but they don't know what. I make my excuses and leave the area sharpish. The boys follow close behind and are greeted by the sight of me on all fours howling with glee. I swear I don't think I ever laughed harder or longer in my life. It takes a good five minutes to explain what I am so curled up about but I eventually manage to blurt out the secret to one of my special cuppas.

"The thing is boys, when I say I made it with my heart and soul, what I really should have said was I made it with my *arsehole,* cos that's where that tea bag has just come from!"

I'm ashamed to say folks, that I had taken that little triangular bag of leafy goodness and inserted it a goodly way up my sweaty bum crack. Then, and this is the crucial part, I had put it into the cup with tepid water first before adding hot water after. This was to ensure the boiling water would not kill the germs I was hoping to pass onto Tegwyn.

"Attention to detail that's what I like about you Crockers" says Gus, with an impressed nodding of the head.

"Good for morale no doubting that", agrees Brewster.

Well suffice to say I didn't have to buy my own beers in the bar that night, after I'd imparted that choice bit of news to the boys. We arrived fresh the next day keen to hear Tegwyn's tales of up all night bum foolery and ring sting. Only thing was, Tegwyn didn't show. We plodded on regardless for the morning and got a lot more done without the aid of our Celtic cowboy. Eventually the news we'd all been expecting came through via Gwyn, the festival director.

"Bad news I'm afraid boys. You might as well take the rest of the day off because, as you will have gathered by now, Tegwyn is not available for work today"

Somehow managing to keep a relatively straight face I enquire after him.

"Oh really Gwyn? Nothing serious I hope?"

'Well apparently, his good lady had to get the doctor out to him last night. Yes, erm it er, seems he let himself down rather badly and er, well, he shit up her back in the middle of the night!"

This news was greeted by uncontrollable mirth.

There was rolling around.

There were cries for mercy.

There was clutching of sides.

There was very nearly the heaving up of breakfast.

And then there was Gwyn.

"Well I never. This won't do. No, no no no no not at all"

I should have known of course that Gwyn would not see the funny side quite as fully as us. After all, he and Tegwyn were related and he was failing quite abjectly, to see the funny side of his brother in law's affliction. It was, let's remember, his beloved sister who'd been so horribly defiled in the middle of the night.

"I must say, that's not the reaction I was expecting. Not. At. All."

I was struggling properly to compose myself then because, after all, a man was ill here with who knows what, and contrary to all the evidence in front of him, Gwyn didn't see it as a laughing matter.

"Yes, laid waste by some sort of faecal infestation of the gut apparently"

That did it again, and Gwyn stalked out of the tent with the sound of hysterical laughter ringing in his ears.

Poor old Tegwyn Jones.


His malady was however, to backfire on me, though not as badly as on his poor wife obviously.

During the four days Tegwyn spent shitting his spine out, I had to take over his duties at the lighting desk. The Festival would start each day at eight o clock and we were in a hotel over forty miles away. The hotels had been booked for us by a lovely lady in the office called Joan. Yes, Joan was lovely alright but she was also bloody useless. She booked hotels for most of our work at the time and she had a dizzying variety of factors that would decide where we ended up staying. Chief among these was whether she liked the sound of the person on the other end of the phone. Other criteria included whether the hostelry had a nice name. Never mind if the place was clean or more pertinently still, had a bar. Never even mind if the hotel or B and B was in the same town or as in this case, even in the same fucking county as the site.

Forty miles would take at least an hour on your average A roads. However, those of you who've driven in Wales will know that forty miles can take anything up to three hours depending on the frequency of "Jones the Tractor" or "Evans the Silage" and their right to;

"Take as long as I want to you bastards"

"Go as slow as I fucking like"

In short, to pootle along the single lane roads at a speed calculated to infuriate any one of the fifty or so cars inevitably dribbling along in their wake. That and the fact that there are a fair few hills to be negotiated in forty Welsh miles added up to a very early start for me and the chaps.

So, it was with a bleary eye and a thick head that I surveyed the bewildering first day's spectacle of The Eisteddfod.

With mouth agape, I struggled manfully to contain my excitement as the first of Cymru's finest strode beclogged onto the stage.

Cerys Mellagellel Dafydd from Bala proceeded to clump heavily around the platform for the next five minutes, in full Welsh costume, stamping her feet and yelping for all she was worth. It was quite puzzling I'll admit. Maybe I was missing the point? Perhaps I, in all my English ignorance, was failing to appreciate the complexities and subtleties involved in this challenging form of dance. Maybe Cerys really was supremely talented and highly skilled. Maybe. But it didn't half look like a little fat kid in fancy dress thumping around having a tantrum. The funny thing is Cerys was then followed by;

Sian, Sioned, Gwen, and Megan who while dressed identically, proceeded to exactly replicate the first performance. It was like some kind of horrific clog based Groundhog Day scenario. I will confess to giving myself over (very disrespectfully) to a few bouts of prolonged giggling, made all the worse obviously, because absolutely no one else found it in the least bit amusing. Why, when it's massively inappropriate, *does* that make it so hard to stop laughing I wonder?

Eventually, after what seemed an age but was in reality a mere forty-five minutes, the competition moved on...and how.

It was now time for the choirs. A massed choir can sound awesome can it not? The Welsh are renowned throughout the world for their choral singing and rightly so. A stirring rendition of Carmina Burana (The Old Spice advert) maybe, or one of the old Welsh favourites like...erm..."Men of Harlech" perhaps or "My My My De-fucking-lilah" or whatever. Any of these would have made a welcome change to the laughable shufflings I'd endured thus far that day. So, it was with the tiniest whiff of expectation I sat back and listened...to six choirs singing the same dirge in the same time and with the exact same tune over and over again! What in holy fuck's name is wrong with these people? I have no idea how many different songs have been written in the eons since we as a species made it down from the trees but it must number in the many tens of thousands surely? Why then did the Welsh at this event seem intent on repeating the *same* dance, the *same* song or the *same* poem ad nauseum? On and on it went until it made this poor fool want to gouge his own eyes out and stick knitting needles in his ears lest he be subjected to this God-awful nonsense any longer?

Four days Tegwyn was off, four fucking days! Which meant four days yours truly had to sit and pay attention to the nonsense listed above. That'll fucking teach me to be a bit more careful who I poison ay?

Well as luck would have it Tegwyn's bowel prevailed in the battle against my amoebic warriors and he duly arrived back on the fifth day, looking none the worse for wear apart from being half a stone lighter. I did him a favour there I'd say and I'm sure he'd want to thank me if I ever had the balls to own up to such an awful deed. In all honesty, once I'd stopped laughing about it, I had actually been worried that I might have gone just a tad too far.

"Morning Tegwyn" I ventured breezily "Tea?"
"Oooooh yes boy...lovely cup of tea, is it?"

Well Tegwyn still wasn't feeling one hundred per cent, so at his request, I stayed in the control booth for the rest of the festival thereby enabling him to take a small "comfort break" when needed. He'd struggled in because as he put it,

"Things will be coming to a head Bard wise, very shortly"

Not the sort of thing any of us would want to miss I'm sure you'll agree.

The poetry competition was really heating up and Tegwyn could barely contain himself such was the febrile atmosphere in the tent. As he never tired of telling me this was the world's...

"Prrrremierr Welsh language poetry competition"

So not to be taken lightly by anyone then!

The prize for the winning poet, or *Bard* to be more precise, was a small amount of cash and a chair. This was not any old common or garden chair though, as Tegwyn was at pains to explain.

"No Crockers, not a Parker Knoll recliner no. No no no no. This is a chair fit for a king! A throne! Yes, a throne hand carved by a master craftsman. Indeed, to God, a magnificent throne, fit for the king of poetry to be crowned upon. Parker fucking Knoll..Ignofuckingrrramus!"

Indeed, this chair was hand crafted and by a master craftsman as it turned out. Only trouble was that it hadn't yet turned up at the festival and with the prize due to be given that afternoon, there were a lot of bums twitching in the organiser's office.

"What do you mean the fucking chair's not even here yet you gibbering idiot!"?

Gwyn was giving it both barrels to "Evans Man", his right-hand man and all round nice bloke. Dabbing his ruddy and profusely sweating face with an already soaking hanky, Evans Man attempted to calm Gwyn down.

"Gwyn Gwyn Gwyn, easy now, don't get so irate man. You'll do yourself a mischief you will, *shout*ing and *carry*ing on all over the place. I'm sure Evans the Wood has it all in hand and is probably pulling up in the car park with it as we speak"

"PULLING UP IN THE CAR PARK EVANS MAN? HOW THE FUCK DO YOU KNOW IF HE'S PULLING UP IN THE FUCKING CAR PARK? HAVE YOU CHECKED OR ARE YOU USING YOUR LEGENDARY POWERS OF ESP?"

This was bawled at high volume no more than an inch from Evans Man's face.

"Gwyn now man really. Calm..."

"DON'T. DO NOT FINISH THAT SENTENCE EVANS MAN. I'LL SWING FOR YOU I SWEAR. JUST GO TO THE CAR PARK AND CHECK IF EVANS THE WOOD HAS INDEED JUST PULLED UP. IF, AS I SUSPECT HE HAS NOT, YOU'RE TO REQUSITION THE FASTEST MOTOR VEHICLE IN BALA, AND TAKE IT AS FAST AS IT WILL GO DOWN TO THAT IDIOT'S WORKSHOP AND

BRING HIM AND THE CHAIR TO ME IS THAT UNDERSTOOD?"

"Gwy..."

"DON'T...SAY ANOTHER FUCKING WORD. JUST GO NOW EVANS MAN, GO LIKE YOU'VE NEVER GONE BEFORE!"

Evans Man made his way out of the office and it was only then that Gwyn noticed Tegwyn and I hovering in the doorway.

"Alright lads? Sorry about that. Evans Man sometimes needs a little bit of encouragement. A *nudge* if you will, in order for him to fully grasp the se*verity* of certain given *situa*tions. Something I can do for you?"

It didn't really seem like the appropriate time to ask when the chair was going to be set on the stage (for us to light it properly) so we made our excuses and went back to our control room.

"Hell of a temper that Gwyn man ey? Wooh! If Evans Man wasn't his cousin I don't think he'd put up with that you know. Lovely man Evans Man fair enough but him and his brother, Evans the Spark, were a bit of a handful in their time oh yes. They'd teach you young bucks a thing or two about fighting...and biting for that matter come to think of it"

I thought better of delving into that last remark any further and to my surprise Tegwyn suggested we all went for a pint.

"As a peace offering you know. Let bygones be bygones ay? Come on now I'll get us all a lovely pint of Brains"

We all trooped off to the onsite refreshment tent and supped a couple of pints of Cardiff's finest, in the dubious company of a half cut local man, who turns out to be none other than the aforementioned Evans the Spark of fighting and biting fame. He is already swaying and slurring his words and it's only half twelve. Good effort.

"Why do they call you Evans the Spark then?" I venture by way of polite conversation.

"You being funny...Pass for comedy that, in England, does it?"

Oh dear. I've obviously offended the man here by asking him a civil question in a language other than Welsh and he has taken an instant dislike to me.

"What does a spark do in England then? Ay? Apart from come up here and nick our jobs that is?"

There's a bit of a back story here, I gather from Tegwyn later, about Evans the Spark and his electricians not getting the contract to do this years' Eisteddfod. Apparently, they've done it every year from year dot but had taken the piss once too often by drinking on site and so had their wrists slapped this year. They were only supplying the generators for this year's event and Evans was here just to perform a maintenance check on them.

"Well, er Evans, was it? Much as I'd like to stand around here and debate the finer points of alcoholism with you, some of us do have gainful employment to go to so I bid you good day. Come on chaps"

At this Evans, the Spark made to grab me but was intercepted by Tegwyn, who placated him by pushing him back into his seat and ordering another beer. We go back via Gwyn's office to ask about the appearance or not thereof of the famed "chair"

"WHAT THE HOLY FUCK DO YOU MEAN BY *DEAD,* EVANS MAN?"

He is shouting as loud as a man can down a phone and has the look of a man teetering on the very brink of a psychotic episode.

"GREAT GOD ABOVE YOU MEAN *ACTUALLY DEAD*...AS IN...UNABLE TO FINISH THE CHAIR DEAD?...WELL IF IT *IS* FINISHED EVANS MAN, GET *IT* IN THE VAN AND GET *IT* BACK HERE A.S.A FUCKING *POSS*IBLE...WE'LL RING A FUCKING AMBULANCE WHEN YOU GET BACK!

There's fuck all to be done for him at this juncture and I'm sure he'd not want all his hard work going to waste by not having the chair here for the ceremony, now would he?"

Gwyn slumped in his seat and visibly deflated. After a few agonising seconds, he turned to us and filled in the gaps on what we were unable to glean from his bellowed conversation with Evans Man.

Evans Man had indeed commandeered the fastest vehicle in Bala and had torn down to Evans the Wood's place. He'd been greeted by and treated to, the site of the venerable sculptor chisel still in hand, dead, slumped in front of a beautiful and more importantly, apparently finished chair.

Gwyn was right I suppose, there was nothing Evans Man could have done for Evans the Wood save offer a brief prayer to the carpenter in the sky maybe. He took Gwyn at his word and loaded the chair carefully into Jones the Meat's van and made his way the ten miles back up the road to the site. This explains why I find Gwyn standing on his chair in his porta cabin looking out the window an hour later, screaming to no one in particular...

"HOW IN GOD'S GREEN LAND CAN IT TAKE EVEN EVANS MAN MORE THAN HALF AN HOUR TO GET FROM LLANTYN TO HERE AY?"

"Excuse me Gwyn is...." I try...

"I ASK YOU HOW? STOPPED OFF FOR A QUICK CUPPA HAS HE? HAVING A CHAT?"

"Gwyn" I say a bit louder.

"WITH THAT MRS OWEN FROM THE *FLORI*STS I'LL WAGER...NOT NOW EVANS MAN! NOT TODAY OF ALL DAYS! YOU'LL BE THE RUIN OF ME. THE FIRST DI*RECTOR* OF THE *FEST*IVAL NOT TO HAVE A CHAIR TO PRE*SENT* TO THE POET..."

*"GWYN!"* I shout.

"Not now Crockers, not a good time"

"Is that not Evans the Meat's van round the back of the stage there now?"

Gwyn stops and looks towards backstage

"What? What? Yes, yes, oh thank the Lord Jesus Christ and all his little cherubs. We are *fuck*ing saved boy!"

I run off after Gwyn as he hurtles out of the cabin, towards the van parked adjacent to the stage and watch as he yanks the door open.

"Evans Man! Evans Man WHERE THE FUCK HAVE YOU..."

But Evans Man is not listening...Evans Man won't hear another thing ever.

Evans Man is as dead as disco.

"All I'm saying is, I'm not touching the fucking thing"

"Don't be silly lad, it's only a chair...A magnificent chair granted, but a chair just the same"

Tegwyn is failing to persuade me or any of the boys to get the chair from the van as poor Evans is carted off, in the back of Bala's second fastest vehicle, to the hospital in Bangor.

Eventually four Druids are coerced into helping and together they and Tegwyn struggle into the tent. It's a big chair this. It really has got a lot of wood in it. It's very finely carved, massively intricate. It must have taken Evans the Wood weeks to do it.

They knock the top clean off it on the frame of the tent door.

There is the biggest intake of breath I have ever heard as the gathered crowd look on and wait to see who is next to be struck down by this "Throne of Doom." But there are no claps of thunder with attendant lightning bolts and no one appears any the worse so they carry on and plonk it, at last in its rightful place, centre-stage. There's only fifteen minutes to go before the audience come back in and we go live on air on BBC Wales to see the crowning of the Bard, live from Bala, at this year's Eisteddfod, brought to you by Huw Edwards and it goes dark. Very dark. The lights have gone off. Bala we have a problem. We've lost power. The malignant chair's curse appears to have struck once more!

All of a sudden it gets serious from my point of view, (not that I was laughing), anyway. Evans Man was by far the pick of the Welsh thus far but this is down to me this. I'm the man in charge of the power, so I pelt out of the tent into the generator compound to see what's going on. I am greeted by the sight of Evans the Spark, pissed as a fart turning the main power breaker on the generator off and on and off and on again.

"What the fuck are you doing!" I yell at him.

"Testing the Fer..ferr..*Fucking break*ers innit" he drools. I grab hold of him by his collar at which point he tries his level best to get my nose in his mouth and my balls in his hand. He succeeds in this second act and I gasp with pain as I throw him off me.

"You English CUNT!" he slurs and comes at me for the second time today. I land what it must be said is a near text book drop kick to his nose which explodes and spews blood and snot over his face and my boot. I give him another right hand for good measure and one more for luck and he drops to the floor and lays motionless, at which point I turn to see Gwyn the festival director looking on aghast at the scene before him.

Sadly, for me and the boys Gwyn did not witness the lead up to my pounding of Evans the Spark, only the act itself.

We didn't do the Eisteddfod again after that...

Can't think why...fucking Druids.

Made in the USA
Lexington, KY
20 April 2017